Rapunzel

An Islamic Tale

For Mawlana Saeed Ur Rahman, the heart and inspiration
behind the Rutter Street Mosque.
Thank you for putting the Qur'an in my father's hand.
I love you, Uncle.

Rapunzel: An Islamic Tale

First Published in 2021 by
THE ISLAMIC FOUNDATION

Distributed by
KUBE PUBLISHING LTD
Tel +44 (0)1530 249230, Fax +44 (0)1530 249656
E-mail: info@kubepublishing.com
Website: www.kubepublishing.com

Author Fawzia Gilani
Illustrator Sarah Nesti Willard
Book design Rebecca Wildman

A Cataloguing-in-Publication Data record for this book is available
from the British Library

ISBN 978-0-86037-734-4
eISBN 978-0-86037-739-9

Printed by Elma Basim, Turkey.

In the name of Allah, the One God, the Most Compassionate, the Most Merciful.

Rapunzel

An Islamic Tale

FAWZIA GILANI

Illustrated by SARAH NESTI WILLARD

Once upon a time, near a thick tangled forest, there lived a husband and wife. They were known for their kindness and generosity and most of all for their happiness. The wife was a clockmaker while her husband worked as a woodcutter. It was the wife's way that with every adjustment of a wheel or spindle she would whisper *bismillah*. It was the husband's way that with every swing of his axe he would say *alhamdulillah*. Every morning they began their day offering Fajr and reading verses from a leather-bound Qur'an.

The couple loved Allah and felt very blessed.

Their cottage was next to a mansion which had a beautiful garden with all sorts of delicious fruits and vegetables. The mansion and garden belonged to a rich but hard-hearted woman known as Shuna Leng who they occasionally saw but only in the darkest hours of the night. Shuna Leng, however, often saw the woodcutter and his wife from one of her many windows. She seethed with jealously whenever she heard the laughter of the wife. Years ago she had hoped that the woodcutter would come to ask for her hand in marriage. But he never did. Instead he won the heart of the happy clockmaker. Shuna Leng had never forgotten and she often wondered how she could create misery in their lives. She constantly wished the very worst for them.

Some months ago the woodcutter and his wife had been blessed with the news of a baby which they hoped would arrive in a few weeks. Every day the wife would stop her work and make sujud asking Almighty Allah to bless her with a kind and generous child. She made constant du'a' throughout the day saying, *"Rabbi hab li min ladunka dhurriyyatan tayyibatan innaka sami'u al-du'a'.* My Lord, grant me from Yourself a good offspring. Indeed, You are the Hearer of supplication." (3:38)

The woodcutter himself would recite verses from Chapter *al-Rahman* as he walked to the forest, and as he chopped and carried wood. He was grateful for his many blessings. Often times he would look up to the heavens and say, *"Fa-bi'ayyi ala'i rabikuma tukadhdhiban.*
So which of your Lord's favours would you deny?" (55:77)
And in response he would take a moment to bow.

After every salah he would say, *"Rabbi hab li min al-salihin,* My Lord grant me from the righteous." (37:100)

Lately the wife had been climbing up to the attic of her cottage and peering through the small window to look at the patch of rapunzel greens growing in Shuna Leng's garden.

As the time for the baby's arrival got closer, the wife's cravings grew stronger. One day the wife's longing for rapunzel greens grew so strong that she said, "Dear husband, I must have some of the rapunzel greens to eat. Please go to Shuna Leng and ask if I may have some."

But the woodcutter advised his wife against it. "*A'udhu billah,* I seek refuge in God," said the woodcutter, "Shuna Leng is a harsh woman, she does not have a generous heart. If I go to her, she will turn me away." But the wife's cravings grew and grew. She urged and implored her husband to get her some rapunzel greens. As the days went by the wife began to grow weaker and weaker. The woodcutter was very worried. In the end, he could not bear to see his wife's anguish any longer, so he went to the mansion and knocked on the door. No one answered.

After every salah the woodcutter went, again and again, but still no one came to the door. Seeing how weak his wife had become the woodcutter went to the mansion in the middle of the night hoping to see Shuna Leng. But no one came to answer the door.

As the woodcutter turned to leave he saw large bunches of rapunzel growing alongside the steps of the mansion. He stooped down and saying, *"Bismillah"* he gathered a clump of leaves. Before he left, he called out, *"As-salaamu 'alaykum* my neighbour, *insha'Allah* I will pay you for this rapunzel." But his words were carried away by the wind and no one came to question him.

The next day the woodcutter took some firewood and some coins and put them at the door of Shuna Leng's mansion as payment for the rapunzel he had taken.

The wife was overjoyed at the sight of the leaves. She ate them up saying *bismillah* with every bite. *Alhamdulillah*, she regained her strength almost immediately. For some days everything went well but it wasn't long before she urged her husband to bring her some more rapunzel.

The woodcutter was afraid that his wife would grow weak so once more he went back to the mansion. Again the woodcutter knocked on the door but no one answered.

He waited a while, then decided to take the rapunzel and return later with the payment. The woodcutter reached down and gathered the leaves. At the very moment that he reached for a second handful he heard a shuffle behind him. He turned quickly to see Shuna Leng. "Thief!" shrieked the woman. "You miserable thief. Coming to my garden and stealing my rapunzel! I will punish you severely."

"Astaghfirullah wa atubu ilayh! Please forgive me dear neighbour." cried the woodcutter. "I will pay you for the greens. My wife is ill and soon to have a baby. She craves rapunzel. I took it for her, I ask you in the name of the merciful Lord who has given you all that you have, please forgive me."

Shuna Leng's eyes pierced the woodcutter but as soon as the baby was mentioned her angry eyes changed. Suddenly her voice became calm and she said, "You can take all the rapunzel you want, but if you have a baby girl you will give her to me. I will take the baby in payment for the stealing of my rapunzel. Agreed?"

The woodcutter was terrified at the words of the woman. With a stammering voice he said, "It is true I took your rapunzel and therefore I must repay you… but how can I give my…"

"Silence!" shouted Shuna Leng as she turned and climbed back up the steps.

As the bitter woman closed the doors to her mansion a sinister smile of satisfaction crept across her face. Finally revenge had presented itself.

When the woodcutter told his wife what had happened his wife collapsed, but once she regained her strength she said, *"Insha'Allah* we will have a boy. *Insha'Allah* everything will be well."

Alas for the wife and her husband, when the baby was born it was a girl. On the very same day Shuna Leng came and took hold of the child. The woodcutter and his wife pleaded and cried but the woman paid no attention to their anguish, their grief or their tears.

"I will name the baby, Rapunzel," declared Shuna Leng. "You took my rapunzel," said the woman with a loud menacing voice as she pushed the woodcutter and his wife away, "And now I will take your Rapunzel."

In a final desperate farewell, the wife thrust the leather-bound Qur'an into Shuna Leng's hands. "Please, I beg of you as the mother of this child," cried the wife, "Please teach my child to love the One who sent this book and its message."

As Shuna Leng carried the baby away, the wife looked up to the heavens and cried, "Dear Allah, please watch over my child, please keep her safe and free from harm. Please my Lord, please restore my child to me!"

And so it was that Shuna Leng took the baby far away from the woodcutter and his wife. Although the woman never harmed the child, neither did she care for her. Instead she ordered her housekeeper, Salsabeel to watch over the baby. "Never ever speak of the woodcutter or his wife," she ordered.

Salsabeel attended to the child's every need. And where the mother's prayers had ended Salsabeel's prayers began. When the baby cried, Salsabeel hurried to comfort her. She would serve only the healthiest food and freshest milk to the little Rapunzel. She shielded the baby from every kind of harm and every kind of distress. Salsabeel loved the child with a mother's heart and in turn the child loved Salsabeel.

The years passed by and Rapunzel grew. Sometimes Shuna Leng summoned the little girl but it was only to say unkind words. If the child laughed or sang, Shuna Leng would scream, *"Silence!"* It was at these moments that the gentle arms of Salsabeel would scoop the child up and hurry her away with soothing whispers.

If things were not bad enough, the child had an unusual quality. She had beautiful, thick hair but strangely it grew at an uncommon rate and whilst this made the child more beautiful, it scorched the jealous heart of Shuna Leng. When she ordered the hair to be cut, the child would become dangerously ill. Salsabeel pleaded for the hair to be left to grow and promised to tend to it.

Rapunzel was older now and understood Shuna Leng's cruelty. The woman did not hide it. But Salsabeel would not let Shuna Leng's evil heart corrupt Rapunzel. She taught the child to be gentle and forgiving, polite and humble, patient and hopeful. Whenever Shuna Leng taunted the child with her cruel words Salsabeel would wipe away Rapunzel's tears.

"Straighten your shoulders my little one," she would say, "Never despair! Make your heart strong! Eschew every painful word with a force of goodness. Remember He is with you wherever you are. *Wa-Huwa ma'akum aynama kuntum*" (57:4). Salsabeel spoke the strengthening words with such fervour and passion. Rapunzel's spirits would lift and the child felt she could overcome anything! At night Salsabeel would take out the leather-bound Qur'an that she kept hidden, *"Insha' Allah*, one day you will return this book to its owners," she would say. When Rapunzel asked who they were Salsabeel would put her finger on her lips and then point to the heavens, and say, "God, He knows, *Allahu a'lam."* (2:216)

Salsabeel narrated the stories of the Prophets, ﷺ. She spoke of their hardship and suffering. She spoke of their mission and trial and most of all about their deep love for God. Rapunzel embraced the stories and etched them deep into her heart. Rapunzel loved studying from the leather-bound Qur'an and gazing up at the sky. It filled her with awe and a deep love for Almighty Allah. Indeed, the woodcutter's daughter was growing up to be the very child that her mother and father had prayed for.

But alas for the poor girl she never stayed very long in one place and this was because Shuna Leng was always wary that the woodcutter might find his child.

It happened that the woman had a fright one day. She sensed that the woodcutter might find his daughter. Salsabeel had been sent on some errands. With no warning the cold-hearted woman took Rapunzel and fled. The only thing the child could grab was the leather-bound Qur'an. Rapunzel cried and pleaded for Salsabeel but ruthless Shuna Leng could not be moved. The loss was too great and should have broken the spirit of one so young, but under the sky were three hearts that sent endless prayers, endless pleas, *subhan' Allah* they never gave up!

Salsabeel's words and ways were tethered to Rapunzel's heart. Not a prayer did she miss, not a day passed by that she didn't turn a page of the leather-bound Qur'an. And with every hateful look, every malevolent word, and every begrudging act that Shuna Leng threw out at the poor child, Rapunzel returned them all with forgiveness and patience.

One day, as the little girl innocently began to give directions to a seamstress on where to bring Shuna Leng's clothes, the woman snapped at her angrily, "No one must know where we live. If anyone finds out, we will have to move again."

"Why must we keep moving? Why must no one know?" asked Rapunzel. But Shuna Leng did not answer. Rapunzel asked again and again until the old woman flew into a rage and thundered, "because of the woodcutter!"

Frightened by the woman's fury, Rapunzel remained silent, but from that moment on she often wondered, *who was the woodcutter?*

Occasionally, Shuna Leng needed to be away for a few days at a time to manage her business matters so she hired a governess to attend to Rapunzel. Rapunzel took an immediate liking to the governess who was named Sidra Tul Muntaha. She reminded her of Salsabeel. Sidra Tul Muntaha never missed her salah and oftentimes awoke to pray tahajjud. The governess quickly understood the harsh ways of Shuna Leng but unlike Salsabeel, she spoke her mind and confronted the woman whenever she could. But Shuna Leng was shrewd, she would cunningly pacify and counter any probing questions the governess had about Rapunzel. Sidra Tul Muntaha did whatever she could to empower Rapunzel, she could see that the girl had a curious gift for making mechanical gadgets. The governess encouraged the child's inventive and creative spirit. She encouraged Rapunzel to take things apart and put them back together. She presented Rapunzel with problems and delighted over the child's successes.

At times Rapunzel would become impatient. The washing and combing of her ever-growing hair was tedious. Sometimes her projects failed, sometimes her calculations were incorrect, she would become frustrated and feel defeated. When this happened Sidra Tul Muntaha would point towards the leather-bound Qur'an.

"And what does it say about patience?" she would ask.

Rapunzel would nod and recite, "'O you who believe! Seek help with patient perseverance and prayer, for God is with those who patiently persevere.' Chapter *al-Baqarah* verse one hundred and fifty-three." Then Rapunzel would smile, look up at the sky, and blow a kiss.

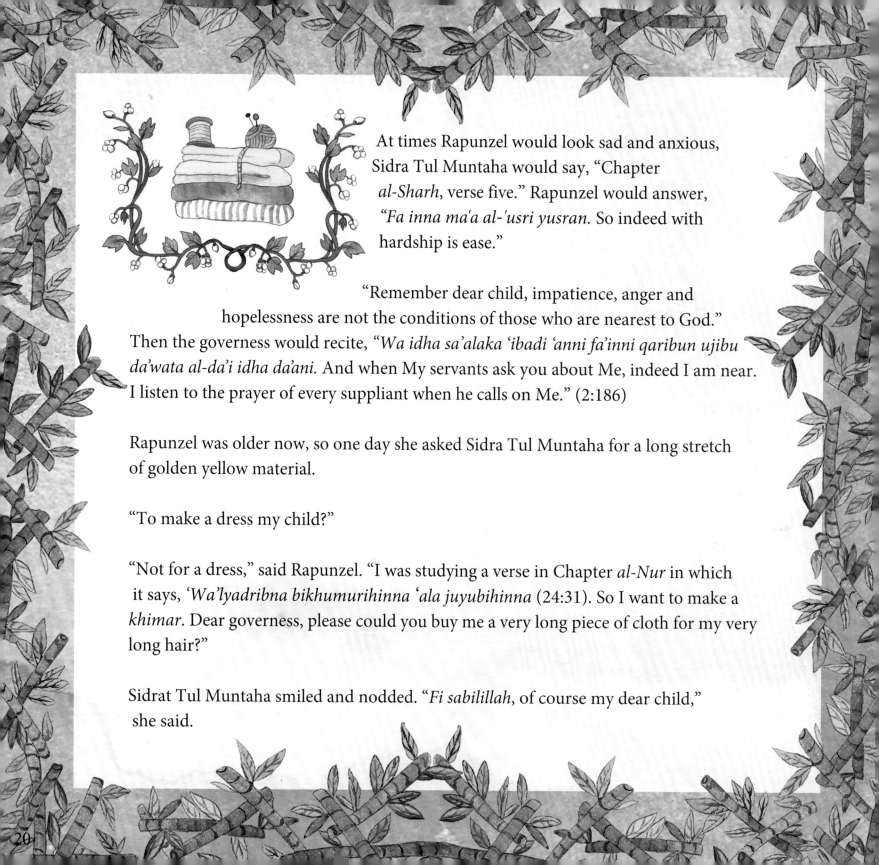

At times Rapunzel would look sad and anxious, Sidra Tul Muntaha would say, "Chapter *al-Sharh*, verse five." Rapunzel would answer, *"Fa inna ma'a al-'usri yusran.* So indeed with hardship is ease."

"Remember dear child, impatience, anger and hopelessness are not the conditions of those who are nearest to God." Then the governess would recite, *"Wa idha sa'alaka 'ibadi 'anni fa'inni qaribun ujibu da'wata al-da'i idha da'ani.* And when My servants ask you about Me, indeed I am near. I listen to the prayer of every suppliant when he calls on Me." (2:186)

Rapunzel was older now, so one day she asked Sidra Tul Muntaha for a long stretch of golden yellow material.

"To make a dress my child?"

"Not for a dress," said Rapunzel. "I was studying a verse in Chapter *al-Nur* in which it says, *'Wa'lyadribna bikhumurihinna 'ala juyubihinna* (24:31). So I want to make a *khimar*. Dear governess, please could you buy me a very long piece of cloth for my very long hair?"

Sidrat Tul Muntaha smiled and nodded. *"Fi sabilillah,* of course my dear child," she said.

One day while Shuna Leng was buying some fruit she heard that a woodcutter was asking about the whereabouts of a child and woman named Leng. The woman dropped the fruit and hurried back to Rapunzel.

"Please dear Shuna, why must we always leave?" asked Rapunzel as she quickly hid her leather-bound Qur'an into a bag.

"Quiet!" said Shuna Leng threateningly. Rapunzel's eyes swelled with tears, "If we must leave then please let us take my governess with us."

"No!" shouted Shuna Leng.

"It's the woodcutter isn't it?" asked the girl. "Silence!" hissed the woman.

Dragging the child she fled far into a forest where she had a hidden tower. Shuna Leng threw Rapunzel into the room at the top of the tower, locked the door and left. Rapunzel stifled her cries and took deep breaths. After a moment she rested her forehead on the ground and whispered the Qur'anic verses that Sidra Tul Muntaha had taught her.

"Be sure We shall test you with something of fear and hunger, some loss in goods, lives, and the fruits of your toil. But give glad tidings to those who patiently persevere. Those who say, when afflicted with calamity, 'To God we belong, and to Him is our return.' They are those on whom descend blessings from their Lord, and mercy. They are the ones who receive guidance." (2:155-157)

The tower was tall and had a long winding staircase which spiraled up to a large room. There was only one window to look out through and only one door to enter. The single key was guarded by Shuna Leng. She always kept it very close to her.

Over time Rapunzel had learned to cope with her seclusion. She remembered everything she had been taught. She repeated the words of her dear Salsabeel, "Never despair! Make your heart strong! Eschew every painful word with a force of goodness. Remember He is with you wherever you are. *Wa-Huwa ma'akum aynama kuntum.*" (57:4)

Sidra Tul Muntaha had said remember God and He will remember you. Rapunzel applied all that she knew. She learned to stay with a problem until she solved it. She learned to complete her tasks no matter how long they took. And she taught herself never to be sad. She began to see every hardship as an opportunity to turn to Allah and gain His pleasure. When a tinge of frustration would enter her heart she would go into sujud and say, "never give up hope of God's mercy, surely no one despairs of God's mercy except those who have no faith." (12:87)

Time passed and Rapunzel's only visitor was Shuna Leng. Rapunzel was always careful not to anger the woman and so she never asked her questions. Instead she asked for books and materials. She knew she could get answers from reading and creating devices kept her mind engaged. The tower room was full of books on every kind of subject. When Rapunzel wasn't reading she would design and experiment with gadgets. Other times she would decorate her room with calligraphy and patterns. It seemed Rapunzel was always busy working on one project or another. But at certain times of the day Rapunzel would lean outside the window, smile at the heavens and say, "This ode is for you dear Allah." Other times she would look down below and say, "Dear world, listen well, these verses are for you." Rapunzel's charming and eloquent voice would echo from one side of the forest to the other and Rapunzel's heart would soar!

Alas one day the key was lost and Shuna Leng could not get into the tower.

"Worry not, dear Shuna," said Rapunzel, as she leaned out the window. "Please wait a few moments, I have an idea. *Insha'Allah* it will work." Rapunzel quickly made a pulley system to hoist up the woman. She threw down her golden yellow scarf and said, "Dear Shuna when you want to come up please say,

> 'Rapunzel, Rapunzel.
> Your long scarf throw here,
> *Insha'Allah* I'll climb up to see you my dear.'"

Shuna Leng let out a snort. Without a word the woman clutched the cloth and let Rapunzel haul her up.

As Shuna Leng looked at the increasing number of gadgets and devices around the room she worried that Rapunzel might be able to open the door without the key, she haughtily informed her that she intended to push a large stone in front of the door. "But why?" asked Rapunzel.

"To keep everyone out," spat out the woman.
"You mean the woodcutter?" asked Rapunzel.
"Who *is* he?"
"The next time you mention the woodcutter it will be the worst for you," threatened Shuna Leng "I will cut off your hair and leave you to perish!"
The woman picked up a plate and threw it at the wall. "Now lower me down," she ordered.

Unknown to Shuna Leng and Rapunzel, living on the other side of the forest was a man, his wife and their two sons, Erkin was six and Ilyar was almost grown. Ilyar spent his time chopping wood and taking it to a market, a day's journey away. Erkin was memorizing verses from Chapter *al-Rahman* but it was taking him a long time.

One day the mother asked Erkin to milk the goats but a baby goat ran off into the forest. Erkin ran after her. When he finally caught the goat he was quite a long way from home. The little boy was tired so he sat down to rest. While he rested he heard the Qur'an being recited. *"Masha'Allah,"* said the boy, "It's Chapter *al-Rahman*."
Erkin quickly got up and began to follow the melodious recitation. Through the trees he saw a tower and in a window high above, he saw a girl.

Suddenly a woman appeared, Erkin quickly hid behind a tree and looked on as the woman walked towards the tower. The woman called out, "Rapunzel, Rapunzel!"

Erkin watched as a long golden yellow cloth tumbled out of the window. He looked in amazement as the woman was pulled up to the window. It was getting late so Erkin returned home carrying his baby goat.

The next day after Erkin had collected the eggs and milked the goats he sat down to learn his verses. When he struggled with his reading he thought of the girl in the tower and wondered if she would help him. He told his parents he would be back soon and trudged through the forest until he reached the tower. Then he shouted up to the girl, "*As-salaamu 'alaykum*."

Rapunzel came to the window and peered at the little boy. "*Wa-'alaykum assalaam*," she replied, "Who are you?"

"I'm Erkin. I'm learning Chapter *al-Rahman*. I heard you reciting it. Would you teach it to me?"

"*Insha'Allah*," said Rapunzel.

The little boy tried to open the door but it was locked. "The door's locked," said Erkin. "And there's a big stone in front of it. It's too heavy to move."

"I know," said Rapunzel with a sigh.

"How do you come out then?" asked the little boy.
"I don't," answered Rapunzel. "I'm not allowed to come out. I always stay inside."

"I saw a woman pulled up with a golden yellow sheet," said Erkin.

"That's my headscarf," said Rapunzel touching the golden yellow cover over her head.
"Hold on to this," said Rapunzel as she threw down her bright long headscarf. *Insha'Allah* I'll pull you up."

"*Jazak Allahu khayran*," said Erkin. The little boy held on tight as he was pulled upwards and then jumped down into the tower room. He looked around and saw beautiful calligraphy decorating the walls, gadgets and contraptions laying neatly on tables and shelves and rows upon rows of books.

"*Masha' Allah*," said Erkin as he looked on in wonder.

Erkin introduced himself to Rapunzel and told her about his family. Rapunzel told Erkin about Shuna Leng and how she came to live in the tower. "You can visit me when you have time and *insha' Allah* I'll help you study Chapter *al-Rahman*," said Rapunzel. "But you must remember that if you are seen visiting me, I will be punished severely."

Over the next few days Erkin visited Rapunzel, listened to stories and practiced his verses. When the little boy's parents heard him recite, they were very surprised. "*Masha' Allah*, you're reciting your verses so well," said his mother.

"*Alhamduliliah*," replied Erkin, "that's because Rapunzel helps me."

"How can rapunzel help you?" asked his father, thinking of the greens.

"She teaches me and she lives in a tower," said the boy. "She's not allowed to come out and if Shuna Leng knows that I visit her, she will hurt her and take her far, far away."
"*Subhan' Allah*," said his mother anxiously. "A tower? Shuna Leng? A girl? This is all very strange. Your brother will be back tonight, *insha' Allah* he will go with you tomorrow."

"No, he mustn't," said Erkin worried. "If the woman sees him, she'll take Rapunzel away and then she won't be able to help me or tell me stories. I like Rapunzel. I don't want her to go away."

The parents looked at each other and said no more. Later that night when Ilyar returned home they shared their concern about a harsh woman and an imprisoned girl.

The next day Erkin went to visit Rapunzel and he warned Ilyar not to go with him. Erkin's mother and father, however, had instructed their older son to find out where the little boy was going. Ilyar followed his brother all the way to the tower and watched Erkin get pulled up to the window and disappear. He could hear Erkin practicing his verses. In the distance he spotted a woman walking towards the tower. A chill ran down Ilya's back. His little brother was in danger and so was the girl.

Today Shuna Leng was moving faster than usual. She had found the key to the tower and was eager to use the stairs but as she came close, she heard Rapunzel and another voice that she did not recognize. The woman's expression changed. A storm of anger raged in her eyes. "How dare she have someone in the tower," screeched the woman. She hurried to the door, removed the large stone, turned the key and rushed inside.

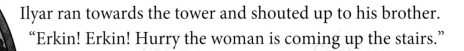

Ilyar ran towards the tower and shouted up to his brother.
"Erkin! Erkin! Hurry the woman is coming up the stairs."

Erkin looked outside the window and Rapunzel peered down.

"She's coming up the stairs. She heard you reciting," shouted Ilyar. "Hurry down!"

Rapunzel immediately threw out her *khimar*. "Quickly, Erkin, use it to climb down," she said.

Suddenly there was a scream.

"Rapunzel! Rapunzel!" shouted Erkin. The little boy was terrified. He clutched Ilyar, "Brother, please we must help her. Shuna Leng will hurt her."

Rapunzel looked bravely at the angry woman. "You have deceived me," Shuna Leng shrieked. "You ungrateful wretch."

"No Shuna Leng, I was helping the little boy recite the Qur'an," cried Rapunzel.

Ilyar looked at Erkin. "Run home as fast as you can and bring Mama and Papa. Tell them to hurry." Erkin ran before Ilyar could even finish his sentence. When Erkin finally got to the cottage, he was so out of breath he could barely speak. He began to cry and pull his parents. The mother and father understood something was wrong and followed their young son through the forest.

Ilyar stood at the bottom of the tower and shouted up.
"*As-salaamu 'alaykum,* Shuna Leng. My name is Ilyar. Please,
I wish to speak with you."

Shuna Leng looked out of the window, her eyes bored into Ilyar.
"I have nothing to say to you. How dare you come to this tower.
Go away and leave us alone," she bellowed.
"I'm not leaving," said Ilyar, "I know who you are," and he sat down
on the ground.

"Impudent boy! You think you know who I am," sneered Shuna Leng. "Who do you think
you are?"

"I'm a woodcutter," said Ilyar holding up his axe. "I chop wood and take it to a town a day's
journey from here. When I go there I sell my wood in a market with another woodcutter.
His wife gives away green rapunzel as a charity."

Shuna Leng looked out of the window and for a few moments stared at Ilyar, then in a fit of
rage she threw a cup aimed at the young man. "Go away!" screeched the woman. "You have no
business here."

"*La hawla wa la quwwata illa billah,*" said Ilyar shaking his head. "Doesn't God say,
'*Waltakun minkum ummatun yad'una ila al-khayr waya'muruna bi'l-ma'rufi wa yanhawna
'ani'l-munkari wa ula'ika hum'l-muflihun.* And let there be among you people inviting to the
good and enjoining the right and forbidding the wrong and those are the successful ones.'"
(3:104)

Shuna Leng threw a dish at Ilyar and screamed when it missed him.

After a time, the man and his wife arrived with Erkin. The wife greeted Shuna Leng and asked her why she had the girl imprisoned in the tower. Shuna Leng's anger grew. In a fitful rage she cut off Rapunzel's hair and snipped the hair and khimar so that it could not be used as a hoist. Then the cruel woman climbed down the stairs and locked the big heavy door. She threw the key into the river. "There!" shouted Shuna Leng as she walked past Erkin and his family, "You'll never save her now. She will die in the tower."

The wicked woman said no more and off she went never to be seen again.

35

Little Erkin shouted up to Rapunzel, "Don't worry *insha' Allah*, we will help you."

Ilyar immediately ran to the door and swung his axe trying to make a hole large enough for Rapunzel to climb through. With every swing of his axe Ilyar whispered *Allahu Akbar*. Rapunzel's hair lay strewn on the floor, she was beginning to feel weak. On hearing the axe against the door, she gathered her tools and leather-bound Qur'an and slowly clambered down the stairs whispering *bismillah* with every step. She called out to Ilyar to stop chopping for a few moments while she set to work on the lock. A few minutes later the door swung open and out stumbled Rapunzel.

Erkin's mother steadied Rapunzel "Please come home with us," she said. The mother nursed Rapunzel back to health and thanked her for teaching her son to recite Chapter *al-Rahman*. Rapunzel thanked the family for their kindness and told them her story and how she had to go in search of her father and mother.

Ilyar looked at Rapunzel and said, "You won't have to search far. I know who your father is. You look just like him." Ilyar pointed north. "His home is a day's journey from here. His wife surrounds their house with rapunzel and gives it freely to everyone who walks by and constantly asks, "Have you seen my Rapunzel? *Subhan' Allah*, I never understood what she meant until now."

Ilyar and his family took Rapunzel to her parents. The woodcutter was selling wood while his wife was holding a basket of greens. She held out a bunch to the girl who stood before her. "Have you seen my Rapunzel?" she asked. Rapunzel's eyes filled with tears as she looked at her mother and held out the leather-bound Qur'an. The basket fell and with a cry the clockmaker instantly clasped her arms around her long lost daughter. The woodcutter came running to embrace his child.

Rapunzel's father and mother held their daughter in their arms and tears of joy ran down their cheeks. "I knew Allah would bring you back to me," whispered the woodcutter's wife, "I never lost hope."

The woodcutter looked up towards the heavens and whispered, "*Fabi'ayyi ala'i rabbikuma tukadhiban.Tabaraka'ismu rabbika dhi'l-jalali wal'-ikram.* So which of your Lord's favours would you deny? Blessed is the name of your Lord, Owner of Majesty and Honour." (55:77-78)

GLOSSARY

Alhamdulillah – Praise be to God.

Allahu Akbar – God is Most Great.

As-salaamu 'alaykum; *Wa 'alaykum as salaam* – Peace be with you/ And on you be peace.

Astagfirullah wa atubu ilayh – I seek forgiveness from Allah and repent towards Him.

A'udhu billah – I seek God's protection.

Bismillah – In the name of God.

Fajr – Pre-dawn prayer.

Fi sabilillah – For the sake of God.

Insha' Allah – God-Willing.

Jazak Allahu Khayran – May God reward your goodness.

Khimar – A veil worn by Muslim women and girls as part of hijab.

La hawla wa la quwwata illa billah – There is no power or might except Allah.

Masha' Allah – God has willed it; said when admiring something or someone.

Qur'an – The Muslim Holy Book revealed to Prophet Muhammad .

Salah – Means 'formal obligatory prayer'.

Subhan' Allah – Glory be to God.

Sujud – Prostration with one's head on the ground, as performed during ritual prayer.

Tahajjud – Voluntary prayer performed after sleeping after the Isha (night) prayer and before the Fajr (pre-dawn) prayer.